Louanne Pig in
Witch Lady

Louanne Pig in
Witch Lady

NANCY CARLSON

Carolrhoda Books, Inc. / Minneapolis

To all my friends
from the old neighborhood

Text and illustrations © 1985 by Nancy Carlson, © 2006 by Nancy Carlson

Carolrhoda Books, Inc.
A division of Lerner Publishing Group
241 First Avenue North
Minneapolis, MN 55401 U.S.A.

Website address: www.lernerbooks.com

Library of Congress Cataloging-in-Publication Data

Carlson, Nancy L.
    Louanne Pig in witch lady / by Nancy Carlson.
      p.   cm.
    Summary: Louanne Pig is befriended by the old woman she always believed to be a witch.
    ISBN-13: 978–0–8225–6196–5 (lib. bdg. : alk. paper)
    ISBN-10: 0–8225–6196–4 (lib. bdg. : alk. paper)
    [1. Friendship—Fiction. 2. Pigs—Fiction. 3. Animals—Fiction.] I. Title: Witch lady. II. Title.
PZ7.C21665Ll 2006
    [E]—dc22   2005032573

Manufactured in the United States of America
1 2 3 4 5 6 – JR – 11 10 09 08 07 06

Everyone knew that the house on top of the hill belonged to a witch.

George had seen her black cat.

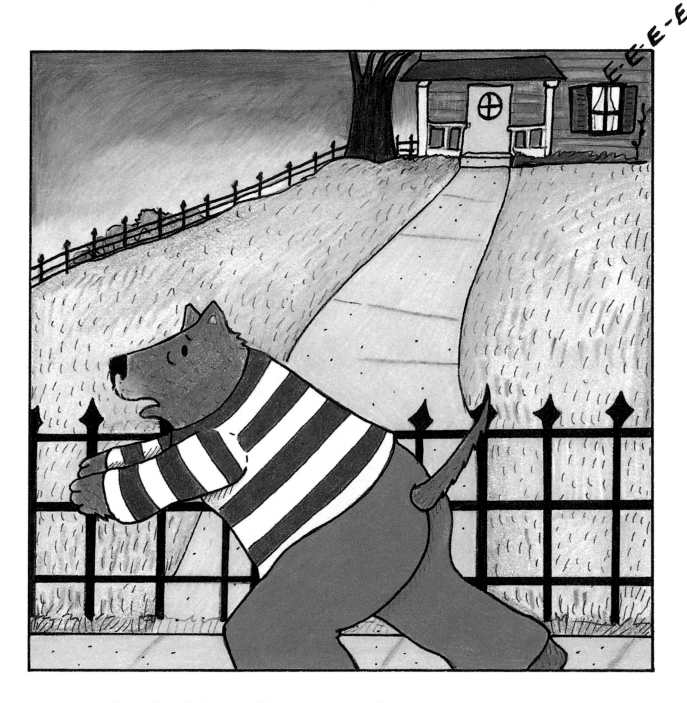

Ralph had heard her screeching at the children
she tortured.

Harriet had once been brave enough to peek
through her dining room window.

"There were tall cages everywhere," she told her friends. "She must be fattening up an awful lot of kids."

Still, every now and then it was fun to cut
through the witch lady's yard.

It made them all feel very brave indeed.

One windy October day, the four friends decided
to prove their courage once again.

They were almost over the fence and safe when
Louanne tripped.

"Owww!" she cried. "I've twisted my ankle. I
can't stand up!"

George and Ralph and Harriet thought about
going back to help their friend . . .

. . . but just as they got up their courage, the
witch lady appeared.

"You naughty children!" she yelled at them.
"Scat!" She clapped her hands.

George and Ralph and Harriet didn't think twice.
They ran like lightning.

The witch lady looked down at Louanne.
"What's wrong with *you*?" she asked. "Be
off with you!"

"I . . . uh . . . I . . . uh . . . I . . . ," Louanne stuttered.

"Spit it out, child," scolded the witch lady.

"I can't," Louanne finally blurted out. "I've twisted my ankle."

"Oh dear," sighed the witch lady. "Well, I can't fix it out here in the cold. There's nothing for it but to come inside."

Louanne knew her goose was really cooked now,
but she had no choice.

The witch lady helped her hobble up the steps
and into the living room.

"Sit here," she said, "while I boil some water."

Oh, no, thought Louanne. She's going to
boil me alive.

Soon the witch lady returned with a plate of
cookies and a cup of tea.

Fattening me up for the kill, thought Louanne.

Then she wrapped cold cloths around Louanne's ankle. In a little while, it felt much better.

"Would you like to see my house?" the witch
lady asked. Louanne nodded. She was beginning
to think they might have been wrong about her.

Upstairs the black cat was curled up in the sun.
"His name is Figaro," said the witch lady. "Go
ahead and pet him." Louanne did. Figaro began to
purr. "He likes you," said the witch lady.

In the dining room were six tall cages. There
were no children locked up in them, though. They
were filled with birds.

"Ohhh," sighed Louanne. "They're beautiful."

Before Louanne left, the witch lady played the piano and sang for her. It did sound a little like screeching.

When Louanne got home, she found George and
Harriet and Ralph on her front steps.

"You're alive!" yelled Harriet.
"How did you ever escape?" asked George.
"You're so brave!" said Ralph.

"I guess I am pretty brave," said Louanne. "In fact, I'm so brave, I think I just might go back there tomorrow. . . .

I forgot to ask her name!"